Dr. M. Jerry Weiss, Distinguished Service Professor of Com-
munications at Jersey City State College, is the educational
consultant for Dragonfly Books. A past chair of the International
Reading Association President's Advisory Committee on Intel-
lectual Freedom, he travels frequently to give workshops on the use
of trade books in schools.

Printed in Hong Kong   10 9 8 7 6 5

Library of Congress Cataloging in Publication Data
Browne, Anthony. Gorilla.
Summary: Neglected by her busy father, a lonely young girl
receives a toy gorilla for her birthday and together they
take a miraculous trip to the zoo.
1. Children's stories, English   [1. Gorillas—Fiction.
2. Fathers and daughters—Fiction]   I. Title
PZ7.B81984Go   1985   [E]   85-13
ISBN 0-394-87525-7 (trade) ISBN 0-394-97525-1 (lib. bdg.)
ISBN 0-394-82225-0 (pbk.)

First Dragonfly edition: February 1989

GORILLA

Anthony Browne

A DRAGONFLY BOOK
Alfred A. Knopf • New York

Hannah loved gorillas. She read books about gorillas, she
watched gorillas on the television, and she drew pictures of
gorillas. But she had never seen a real gorilla.

Her father didn't have time to take her to see one at the
zoo. He didn't have time for anything.

He went to work every day before Hannah went to school,
and in the evening he worked at home.

When Hannah asked him a question, he would say, "Not now.
I'm busy. Maybe tomorrow."

But the next day he was always too busy.
"Not now. Maybe on the weekend," he would say.
But on the weekend he was always too tired.
They never did anything together.

The night before her birthday, Hannah went to bed tingling with excitement—she had asked her father for a gorilla!

In the middle of the night, Hannah woke up and saw a very small parcel at the foot of the bed. It *was* a gorilla, but it was just a toy.

Hannah threw the gorilla into a corner with her other
toys and went back to sleep.

In the night something amazing happened.

Hannah was frightened. "Don't be frightened, Hannah," said the gorilla, "I won't hurt you. I just wondered if you'd like to go to the zoo."

The gorilla had such a nice smile that Hannah wasn't afraid. "I'd love to," she said.

They both crept downstairs, and Hannah put on her coat. The gorilla put on her father's hat and coat. "A perfect fit," he whispered.

They opened the front door and went outside.

"Come on then, Hannah," said the gorilla, and he gently lifted her up. Then they were off, swinging through the trees toward the zoo.

When they arrived at the zoo it was closed, and there was a high
wall all around. ''Never mind,'' said the gorilla. ''Up and over!''
    They went straight to the primates. Hannah was thrilled.
So many gorillas!

The gorilla took Hannah to see the orangutan, and a chimpanzee. She thought they were beautiful. But sad.

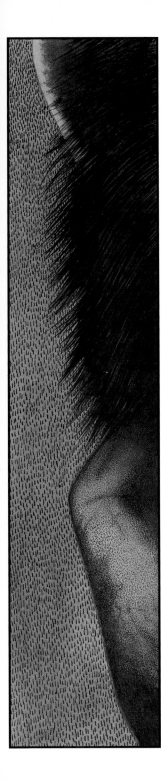

"What would you like to do now?" the gorilla asked.

"I'd love to go to the movies," said Hannah. So they did.

Afterward they walked down the street together. "That
was wonderful," said Hannah, "but I'm hungry now."
"Okay," said the gorilla, "we'll eat."

"Time for home?" asked the gorilla.

Hannah nodded, a bit sleepily.

They danced on the lawn. Hannah had never been so happy.

"You'd better go in now, Hannah," said the gorilla. "See you tomorrow."

"Really?" asked Hannah.

The gorilla nodded and smiled.

The next morning Hannah woke up and saw the toy gorilla. She smiled.

Hannah rushed downstairs to tell her father what had happened.
"Happy birthday, love," he said. "Do you want to go to the zoo?"
Hannah looked at him.

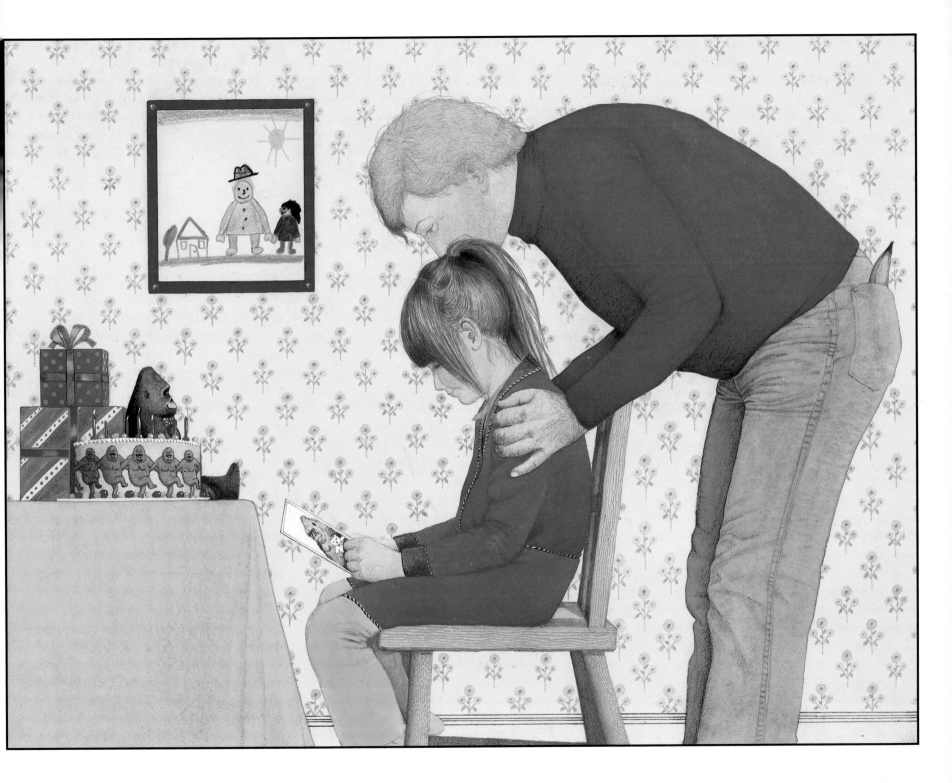

She was very happy.